For my grandson Ruairidh—
Happy Second Christmas, with love
– D H

For Jim (Big Mouse) and Raechele (Little Mouse)
– J C

This edition produced 2008 for BOOKS ARE FUN LTD
1680 Hwy 1 North, Fairfield, Iowa, IA 52556

Copyright © 2005 tiger tales, 202 Old Ridgefield Road, Wilton, CT 06897
International Standard Book Number: 978-1-84506-913-1

Text copyright © Diana Hendry 2005
Illustrations copyright © Jane Chapman 2005

Original edition published in English by Little Tiger Press,
an imprint of Magi Publications, London, England, 2005.

Printed in China

Library of Congress Cataloging-in-Publication Data is available for this title.

The Very Snowy Christmas

Diana Hendry

Jane Chapman

It was Christmas Eve.
Big Mouse was making
cheese pies. Little Mouse
was making paper chains.
"Merry Christmas to us!
Merry Christmas to us!"
sang Little Mouse. "Big
Mouse, can I decorate
the Christmas tree now?
Can I? Can I?"

"We'll do it together," said Big Mouse.

Little Mouse hung golden acorns and mistletoe berries on the tree.

Big Mouse put a star on the top.

"But we forgot the holly!" cried Little Mouse. "I'll go and get some." And off he ran.

"Make sure it has nice red berries!" called Big Mouse.

Little Mouse set off down the path singing, "Jolly holly! Holly jolly! Jolly holly Christmas!"

But there was no holly to
be seen on the first corner.

And no holly on
the second corner.

And no holly on
the third corner.

So over the bridge ran
Little Mouse…and at last
he found a holly bush with
shiny red berries! He jumped
up and down with excitement.

"Oh jolly holly! Holly jolly!
Jolly holly Christmas!" sang
Little Mouse, stretching high
on his toes to reach some.

But suddenly, soft white flakes began falling
all around him. One flake fell on Little Mouse's
nose and made him sneeze. "Goodness me!"
said Little Mouse. "The sky is coming undone!"

As Little Mouse hurried home, many more pieces of sky fell down upon him. Faster and faster they fell. They fell on his ears and his whiskers and his tail.

"Oh dear, oh dear," said Little Mouse. "I'd better take some of this home to show Big Mouse. He'll know how to stitch the sky together again."

Little Mouse made a ball of white flakes and put it in his bucket. Then back over the bridge he hurried.

Suddenly, he saw a strange creature
in the water, making faces at him!
It had lots of ears and a blurry face,
and it waved its arms at Little Mouse.

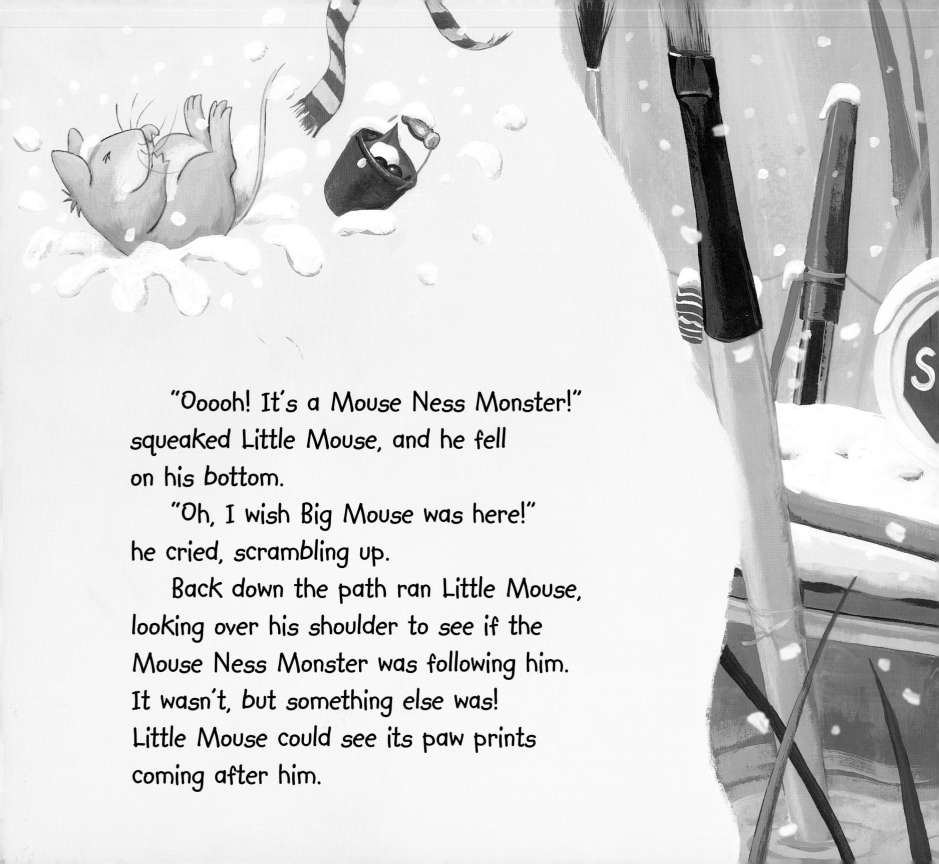

"Ooooh! It's a Mouse Ness Monster!" squeaked Little Mouse, and he fell on his bottom.

"Oh, I wish Big Mouse was here!" he cried, scrambling up.

Back down the path ran Little Mouse, looking over his shoulder to see if the Mouse Ness Monster was following him. It wasn't, but something else was! Little Mouse could see its paw prints coming after him.

"EEEEKKK! HELP! EEEEKKK!"
squeaked Little Mouse. "Now there's
an Invisible Monster chasing me!"

Little Mouse ran up and down
and around and around in circles
to escape, but the paw prints of the
Invisible Monster went up and down
and around and around after him.

Little Mouse ran and ran.
Faster and faster whirled
the white flakes and faster
and faster ran Little Mouse.
And still the Invisible
Monster followed him.

At last, Little Mouse saw his house.
But there in the garden was a huge
White Mouse!
"Oh no, no, no!" squeaked Little
Mouse. "Another monster waiting
to catch me!"
Little Mouse trembled
and began to cry.

But then the front door opened and there was Big Mouse. Little Mouse leapt into Big Mouse's arms.

"Big Mouse, Big Mouse!" he cried. "The sky has come undone! And look!" he wailed, pointing to the paw prints. "An Invisible Monster has been following me, and there was a terrible Mouse Ness Monster in the water, and now that scary White Mouse is staring at me!"

"Oh Little Mouse," said Big Mouse,
"the sky hasn't come undone.
It's SNOWING!

"And there aren't any
monsters. Those are your
paw prints.

"And that Mouse Ness Monster
was your reflection in the water.
Look!" And Big Mouse showed
Little Mouse his face in a puddle.

"And this is a snow mouse I made to welcome you home," he said. "Let's make another." And so they did!

"Snow is magic!" cried Little Mouse.
"Yes," said Big Mouse. "Santa Claus likes snow, too!"
Little Mouse jumped up and down. "Will he be here soon? Can I hang up my stocking now?"
"You can," said Big Mouse. "Let's go and get warm first."

So in they went and warmed their paws by the fire.

Little Mouse hung up his stocking and Big Mouse hung up his stocking, too. The holly berries shone in the firelight.

"It's almost Christmas," said Little Mouse. "Holly jolly, jolly holly Christmas!" And he wiggled his warm toes.